Inspire the WORLD

A Kid's Journey to Making a Difference

Words by
Sammie
Vance

Doodles by
Talitha
Shipman

I dedicate this to kids who want to make a difference
but don't know how to start.
-Sammie

What started as 8-year-old Sammie Vance's mission to get a buddy bench for her school to fight loneliness grew to be so much more. Now Sammie is making a difference beyond her hometown. In her first-ever book, Sammie shares how she's encouraging others through recycling, community, giving, determination, bravery, helping, being herself, and celebrating. She wants to inspire the world one kid at a time.

Clear Fork Publishing
P.O. Box 870 102 S. Swenson Stamford, Texas 79553 (915) 209-0003
www.clearforkpublishing.com

Printed in the United States of America

Graphic Design & Page Layout by
Nicolle Ginter of VimAnnVigor Design
vimannvigor.com • @vimannvigordesign

Hardcover ISBN - 978-1-950169-58-0

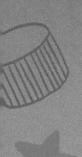

Table of Contents

HELLO

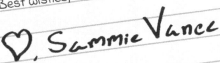

CAPTASTIC

Hello friends,

I'm Sammie Vance, and I'm 12 years old. Are you older or younger than me? The great thing is that age doesn't matter. one thing I've learned: you don't have to be an adult to make a difference in the world!

You can inspire others. Just like I did. My journey started on the playground when I noticed a lot of lonely kids. I wanted to fix that and create more friendships. So, I did exactly that. But then, something amazing happened. Where I had thought my journey would end, it turned out to be just beginning.

My one-cap-at-a-time act of kindness spread across the country. I inspired others through recycling, community, giving, determination, bravery, helping others, being myself, and celebrating.

MY DEFINITION OF INSPIRE: FILL SOMEONE WITH THE DESIRE TO MAKE A DIFFERENCE AND DO SOMETHING GOOD.

I hope my story will do just that. I hope it helps start you on your own journey of Inspiring the World!

Best wishes,

♡. Sammie Vance

Inspire
THROUGH
Recycling

WHAT'S IN THOSE
63 BAGS?

PLASTIC CAPS
& LIDS

THANK YOU

RECYCLED = FRIENDS & MORE

3

I heard about the buddy bench at summer camp a few years ago. When someone is lonely, they can sit on the bench and others know to ask them to play.

It was a solution to my problem. A way to help create friendships and to show kindness. I had no idea how to "make" a buddy bench, but I knew my school needed them. So, I asked for help.

BENCH BRAINSTORM

Wrought Iron ← Too Fancy!

Steel

Might Rust! →

Wood

splinters!

With my mom's help, I found a company called Green Tree Plastics. They make benches out of recycled plastic caps and lids.

Buddy benches made from recycled plastic are sturdy and durable. Unlike wood benches that can splinter and metal benches that rust.

Recycling, helping the planet, and preventing loneliness all in one. Perfect!

Now I needed lots and lots of plastic caps and lids. I began to recycle everything at home, but it wasn't enough.

BUDDY BENCH

CAPS

Q: WHY JUST PLASTIC CAPS & LIDS?

A: Because plastic caps and lids for a long time couldn't be recycled but then Green Tree found a way to reuse them! They grind them up, melt them, and put them into molds.

I made a board of examples. There are lots of different types of caps and lids you can use.

Fun Fact: I have my own Buddy Bench from Green Tree Plastics in my backyard. I love seeing the bits of colorful caps in it!

HOW CAN YOU RECYCLE AND MAKE A DIFFERENC

Inspire
THROUGH
Community

I needed lots of plastic caps and lids.

I needed lots of **HELP**!

A whole community of help.

Using creativity is a perfect way to get a community involved.

How did I use creativity?

I drew a comic.

And put it up **EVERYWHERE**!

BUT I DIDN'T STOP THERE

CAPTASTIC!

My mom made a video of me asking others for help collecting plastic caps and lids. I also asked my school, PTA, local pharmacies, coffee shops, TinCaps baseball team, and anyone else I could think of!

And it worked!

The project took off!

My comic + video + everyone spreading the word = HELP! I received plastic caps and lids from all over the country.

Even internationally!

handfuls

bags

barrels!

And because of everyone's help, I collected enough caps and lids for three buddy benches; in just two months!

I learned that the world is ONE big community that can come together for anything.

And because of global community, kids and adults all over the world have buddy benches.

9

PROCESS Q&A

Q: WAS GETTING THE WORD OUT HARD?

A: No! But it took time. I brought my comic to many places and explained why I was collecting plastic caps and lids and asked if they would help. Every week my mom and I would go to local businesses to pick up what they collected.

MAP OF THE UNITED STATES

my cap map

To: Sammie Vance
From: Mr. Pi's English Class. ☺

Fun Fact: I received caps from all fifty states! And all around the World! These are from Mexico.

HOW CAN YOU INVOLVE THE COMMUNITY?

Inspire
THROUGH
Giving

323 pounds of caps sorted & ready to be recycled into buddy benches!

I gave lots of time to this project. Sometimes I missed things I wanted to do like watching a movie or going to a party. But it is important to give your time for something that will help others.

And for something that you believe in.

Experiencing our world as one BIG community...

I am so grateful to everyone. For caps and lids, working and sorting them, the endless hours of time, and the donations of money. Thank you!

Because of community, we've inspired more community.

There are many ways to give.

And not just with donating money.

Food, toys, clothes... This list can be endless.

People GAVE a lot of caps and lids.

People GAVE a lot of time.

Troop 20202

My Girl Scout troop helped sort caps and lids during a meeting.

PROCESS Q&A
Q: HOW DO YOU SORT CAPS AND LIDS?

A: After collecting caps, sorting is the next step. Sorting is making sure there are only plastic caps going in the bag to be weighed (no metal, paper, or bottles). You do not have to sort by color or type. My favorite way to is to get a group together to sort and weigh the caps. You will get done faster too. Sometimes we put on fun music.

Fun Fact:

I was able to give 7 buddy benches to schools in Indiana thanks to Walgreen' collecting caps for r all summer! Impacti over 40,000 kids!

HOW CAN YOU GIVE?

Inspire
THROUGH
Determination

ONE CAP at a TIME!

DETERMINATION = TO KEEP GOING AND NEVER GIVE UP

People told me my project would take a long time. They didn't want me to be discouraged if it took months or even years to collect enough caps...

My goal was 400 lbs!
(about 10 "55 gallon" drums worth)

I was up for the challenge and very determined.

Then caps and lids started pouring in. My dad told me it would probably slow down but instead...

It sped up!

As each drum filled, I colored in a part of a picture of the buddy bench so everyone at school could see the progress we were making.

I made school announcements to encourage everyone to keep collecting. It was fun.

I didn't give up!

Q: HOW DO YOU KNOW WHEN YOU HAVE ENOUGH CAPS TO GET A BUDDY BENCH?

A: You weigh as you go! Weigh yourself then weigh yourself with a bag of sorted caps. Find the difference! Write it down. On to the next bag.

One 6 ft. Buddy Bench weighs 200 lbs and is made of about 18,000 plastic caps and lids!

you can fit over 3,000 caps into one trash bag

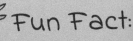

Fun Fact:

I made a $50 bet with my dad at the beginning of the project. He said it would take a year to complete! Boy was he wrong! And he loved being wrong! He thought it would take a year to collect enough for one buddy bench, we got enough for three in two months!

my dad

WHAT ARE YOU DETERMINED TO ACCOMPLISH?

Inspire THROUGH Bravery

BRAVERY = DOING SOMETHING THAT SCARES OR INTIMIDATES YOU

19

I became brave by learning to be less shy. I spoke to other kids and adults about kindness, the buddy bench, and about my journey.

During my first news interview, I was so scared. My voice was barely a whisper. What I wanted to say was important, so I practiced.

A lot!

After a few more interviews I was more confident. My mom said I was even better than her. Learning to be brave allows us to inspire others to be brave.

My School

Store Managers

I practice my speeches over and over again. I recite it in front of my parents and with my sister at night in bed.

I am always open for advice on how to improve. I used to look down at my written speech when addressing a crowd. Now I look out to the audience and think of the impact I can make.

When I am onstage I sometimes get nervous. The lights are so bright I can't see anyone. I wonder if the microphone will pick up the shaking in my voice.

The Today Show = Lots of Cameras

o to EEP lready!

However once I start to talk I calm down and soon my words seem to flow and I am in my happy place.

Now I'm excited to speak!

21

PROCESS Q&A

Q: HOW CAN YOU PREVENT STAGE FRIGHT?

A: Know beforehand what you want to say and practice. Remember why you are speaking and who your audience is. If your mind goes blank, it's ok! Take a deep breath and try again.

Fun Fact:

There is a special award named for me. It is the IJA Sammie Vance Youth Civic Achievement Award.
It will be given to others who are making a difference for years to come! Maybe you could win it someday!

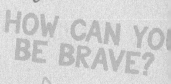

Check out my speech on page 37

HOW CAN YOU BE BRAVE?

Inspire
BY
Being Yourself

Be Kind!

Since I started my project four years ago I have changed quite a bit but in a good way. Physically I have gotten taller and my glasses have changed. Please note: Freckles have remained the same.

I am more confident. I am braver. But I am still me. I have the same goals, dreams, and heart as before. I still want to make a difference every day. I still don't want to see anyone lonely. And I continue to pick up plastic caps and lids.

Know who you are and be happy with it. Be willing to speak up and speak out for what is important to you because you are the best one to do it! You are the only you.

Even though I keep busy with my project and finding fun ways to spread kindness, I make time for just being a kid too.

I enjoy many things. I love hanging out with my friends, eating pizza, family games, playing piano, sketching, and school. My favorite subject is math.

I find it fun to be creative.

I made my comic come to life.

PROCESS Q&A

Q: WHAT ARE SOME THINGS YOU HAVE DONE THAT 8 YEAR OLD SAMMIE WOULD NOT HAVE THOUGHT POSSIBLE?

A: 8 year old me would not have thought that today Sammie would have spoken on stage, been interviewed for TV, Newspapers and Magazines, helped over 150 groups get a buddy bench, lead kindness campaigns, start her own podcast, and write a book that would be published! I have learned through this journey that I can be and do anything I put my mind to.

Fun Fact:

I am really good at hula hooping! When I was 5 I picked one up and have been considered "Queen" ever since. I can hula hoop while walking, talking, reading, and even eating.

MY SUPERPOWER IS KINDNESS! WHAT IS YOURS?

Inspire

THROUGH
Helping
Others

Jury & Pool

CAPTASTIC!

I have helped a lot of people over the past few years!

I have donated thousands of pounds of caps to other groups starting their own buddy bench project.

I love to pay it forward.

I now help other schools kick off their own collection by sending a video and letters of encouragement.

I have met so many new friends. I receive videos and letters from kids and adults all over the US and even the world.

Check out this shirt!
Sent from a school
in Arizona.

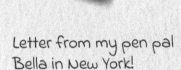

Every Cap Counts!

Just like every act of
kindness counts.

Letter from my pen pal
Bella in New York!

(I was able to help her
get her buddy
benches.)

Some groups I've
helped even send me
cool shirts from their
school or gifts with my
comic on it.

PROCESS Q&A
Q: HOW MANY PEOPLE HAVE I HELPED?

A: Kids ask all the time how many caps I have collected and how many people I've inspired! I don't know the exact number. I do know that I have collected millions of caps with the help of others. It's a team effort. I have been able to assist hundreds of groups and schools get buddy benches. If one kid makes a new friend because of it, that makes me happy.

Fun Fact:

With the help of UPS, I was able to fund the shipping of caps and delivery of buddy benches to 13 groups in 12 states in the US!

HOW CAN YOU HELP OTHERS?

Inspire BY Celebrating

Once I collected enough caps, I discovered that I had enough for three buddy benches for my school. I threw some caps up in the air and did a "**Cap Dance**".

Yahoo Now
Thursday at 5:35 PM · 🌐

Adorable Sammie Vance collected over 1,200 lbs of recycled bottle caps and turned them into 'Buddy Benches' for her classmates 👫 ❤ 👫

HEIDI VANCE

YAHOO! NOW

WAY TO GO, SAMMIE!

FACEBOOK WATCH
Little girl invents 'Buddy Benches' so kids

It is ok and important to take time to celebrate once you reach a goal.

When my school's buddy benches arrived, we had an assembly with the students and an open house for the public to celebrate and to thank everyone for their help.

I wanted everyone to see the result of their hard work!

I love to celebrate with other groups that have done the project. Sometimes they send photos of their finished buddy benches, or I am invited to come to their school and meet them. Other times I send a video.

PROCESS Q&A

Q: HOW OFTEN DO YOU CELEBRATE?

A: Reaching the end goal is just one reason to celebrate! I had many milestones along the way. From filling the drum full of caps for the first time; getting enough caps for one, two, and three benches; getting caps from all fifty US states; giving away seventy-five buddy benches; hearing that another group got their buddy bench; making a new friend! Celebrating is fun! Keeping people excited with you along the way is fun! I have done many cap dances.

Fun Fact:

I have a jar of caps that I keep that are from other states. I like doing cap art with them to celebrate different holidays.

Guess how many caps are in this jar?
*answer on pg 44

HOW WILL YOU CELEBRATE?

Inspire THE World !

I feel honored that I have made connections all over the world!

I did not do this project to be in the news or win awards. I just did it to help others make friends.

I don't know what makes a video viral but videos that include my project have been viewed over 40 million times. I bet my mom is probably 1 million of the views.

There are 33 countries represented on my Facebook page.

Groups as far away as India, Australia, Mexico, and Germany have asked how they can start their own buddy bench project.

I hope my story has inspired you to make a difference.

Recycle
Involve community
Give
Stay determined
Be brave
Help others
Be yourself and
Celebrate!

WHAT AMAZING
JOURNEY
WILL YOU TAKE?

Be Kind!

Mine started with a dream of a buddy bench for my school and a recycled plastic cap!

IJA Welcome show speech by Sammie Vance

Hello Ladies and Gentlemen,

I am honored to be here tonight.

I heard about a buddy bench 2 years ago and thought it was a great idea and my school needed it!

A buddy bench is a tool for when someone is lonely, they can sit on the bench and another person can ask them to play.

I did this for my school in a unique way because, my buddy benches made out of recycled plastic caps that were collected and then made in the benches. I did this to recycle, help the planet, help the animals survive and help prevent loneliness all in one.

I did not do this to be on TV or in the newspaper or even to go to New York City. Honestly, I had no idea that any of this would happen. I did this to help people make friends.

With the communities' help, I was able to collect enough recycled plastic caps and lids for 3 buddy benches in 2 months (about 1,200 lbs) with extras left over to help other schools get started!

In the past year, I have been able to help get over 100 schools buddy benches in the US! Now people all over the world are wanting to do the project. From India to Australia and Germany to Mexico.

I am so happy others all over the world are now wanting to get buddy benches.

You don't just have to be an adult to make a difference, you can be a kid too!

Everyone deserves to have at least one good friend.

You can make a huge change in the world, every single one of you! Mine started with just one cap.

If you can Dream it you can Do it.

Thank you for having me and for this award!

38

Ladies and Gentlemen!

Sammie's Cap Poem

Caps are here Caps are there
Cap talks here Cap talks there
CAPS CAPS everywhere
Caps in my hair
Caps stuck on my clothes
Caps Caps are everywhere
Caps from cities Caps from States
Caps from you
Caps from me
Caps are in my dreams
Filling Drums Sorting Caps
Day after Day more caps more caps I see
It makes me Happy Yippee!!!

Fun Fact

I was 8 when I wrote this poem and read it during one of my Facebook live "Cap Talks". I was very excited about all the caps coming in.

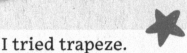

Little known things about Sammie

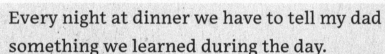

I tried trapeze.

Every night at dinner we have to tell my dad something we learned during the day.

I am a very picky eater.

I ran one 5k and wore a Wonder Woman Costume. (3rd grade)

My cousin was born one day from me and I share the same birthday with her mom.

I make a really good apple pie, which is also my favorite dessert.

I made a buddy bench for my dolls. (3rd grade)

Nicole is both my sister and my middle name.

I composed the intro music for my podcast Sammie Smiles.

I have been to Mexico.

In 2nd grade I won first place in a poetry contest.

I have a dolphin made out of caps just like the buddy bench is. I named it Caperie.

Favorite Animal: Giraffe

Favorite Color: Teal, Aqua

Favorite Food: Cheese Pizza

Do you have any nicknames: My full name is Samantha but most everyone calls me Sammie. I have also been called Cap Girl, Buddy Bench Girl and Kindness Guru

Who Inspires you: My Parents, Malala Yousafzai, & Lin-Manuel Miranda

Favorite Season: Fall, Spring

Do you have any pets? No because my brother is allergic, and my mom says she has 4 kids and that is enough

How many sisters or brothers do you have? One older brother and a younger brother and sister

Favorite outdoor activity: Sidewalk Chalk Art

Favorite Drink: Coca Cola

What do you want to be when your grow up? I am not sure. Possibly Mayor, President, or Journalist. I know I want to do something that I can help people

What inspired you to write a book? I wanted to encourage and inspire other kids that they can make a difference no matter their age and when you see a real-life example that can help motivate.

What awards have you received for what you do: Certificate of Excellence, Action for Nature Eco Hero Award, Youth Service Award, Daily Points of Light, ACEM Environmental Award, IJA Sammie Vance Youth Civic Achievement, Kiwana's, Diana Award, Gloria Barron Prize for Young Heroes, Prudential Spirit of Community Award

Please note that getting awards are nice and allow me to spread my message further but meeting others, helping people, and spreading kindness is the best part.

www.sammiesbuddybenchproject.com

Met my city's Mayor

On set with UPS

Green Tree Plastics
ABC Promise Partnership
&
Walgreens
Trusted since 1901

Sammie's Buddy Bench Project

Welcomes Sammie

Green Tree Plastics tour-see how buddy benches were made

Be Kind!

Highlights Gallant Kid

Song written for me by
Kathie Lee Gifford
on the Today Show

KLG & HODA

on TV show Operation Awesome – my episode Kindness Counts

Pen pals from around the world

Cap Art!

You Don't Have To Be An Adult To Make A DIFFERENCE. You Can Be A Kid Too!!
— SAMMIE V.

How can you recycle and make a difference?

How can you involve the community?

How can you give?

What are you determined to accomplish?

How can you be brave?

My superpower is kindness, what is yours?

How can you help others?

How will you celebrate?

What amazing journey will you take?

Connect with Sammie

sammiesbuddybenchproject.com
Facebook: Sammie's Buddy Bench Project
Instagram: @sammiesbuddybenchproject
Twitter: @SammieBenches
YouTube: Sammie Smiles

*Jar of Caps answer:
500 caps

Sammie Vance lives in Fort Wayne, Indiana with her parents and 3 siblings. She loves school and a good book she can get lost in. Sammie loves meeting new people and finding out what makes them smile. She is best known for spreading kindness through recycling plastic caps into buddy benches.

Sammie has been a guest on the Today Show and partnered with big companies like Walgreens and UPS who were inspired by her mission. She has won numerous awards for her buddy bench project and volunteering efforts. Sammie hopes this book will inspire others to make a difference no matter their age. This is Sammie's first book.

Sammie and Talitha at Sammie's elementary school buddy bench

Talitha Shipman is a children's author and illustrator born and raised in Indiana. Her favorite subjects to paint are wild kids and wild animals. She is inspired by nature and hopes her work encourages curiosity in all ages.

Talitha's books include the Sidney Taylor Honor book, *Everybody Says Shalom* by Leslie Kimmelman (Random House Books for Young Readers, 2015), *Applesauce Day* by Lisa Amstutz, an American Farm Bureau Recommended Read (Albert Whitman, 2017), and most recently, *Finding Beauty*, her first author/illustrator picture book (Beaming Books, 2021).

She lives in Fort Wayne, Indiana with her husband Michael, her daughter Coral, and her pup Indy.

CPSIA information can be obtained
at www.ICGtesting.com
Printed in the USA
LVHW070301180821
695559LV00001B/6